WONDER WOMAN
★ THE AMAZING AMAZON ★

CIRCE'S DARK REIGN

WRITTEN BY
BRANDON T. SNIDER

ILLUSTRATED BY
LUCIANO VECCHIO

WONDER WOMAN CREATED BY
WILLIAM MOULTON MARSTON

DC SUPER HEROES

STONE ARCH BOOKS
a capstone imprint

PUBLISHED BY STONE ARCH BOOKS IN 2018
A CAPSTONE IMPRINT
1710 ROE CREST DRIVE
NORTH MANKATO, MINNESOTA 56003
WWW.MYCAPSTONE.COM

CATALOGING-IN-PUBLICATION DATA IS AVAILABLE AT THE LIBRARY OF
CONGRESS WEBSITE.
ISBN: 978-1-4965-6530-3 (LIBRARY BINDING)
ISBN: 978-1-4965-6534-1 (PAPERBACK)
ISBN: 978-1-4965-6538-9 (EBOOK PDF)

SUMMARY: DURING A BATTLE WITH THE SERVANTS OF EVIL,
WONDER WOMAN RECOVERS A PIECE OF AN ANCIENT WAND. WHEN SHE
DISCOVERS THE ARTIFACT IS INFUSED WITH DARK MAGIC, SHE SETS
OUT TO FIND THE REMAINING PIECES BEFORE THEY FALL INTO THE
WRONG HANDS. LITTLE DOES SHE KNOW, CIRCE ALSO HAS HER EYES
ON THE POWERFUL PRIZE. CAN WONDER WOMAN SECURE THE WAND
BEFORE IT'S TOO LATE? OR WILL CIRCE'S SORCERY REIGN SUPREME?

EDITOR: CHRISTOPHER HARBO
DESIGNER: HILARY WACHOLZ

Printed and bound in Canada.
PA020

TABLE OF CONTENTS

With countries in chaos and the world at war, Earth faced its darkest hour. To answer its cry for help, the Amazons on the secret island of Themyscira held a trial to find their strongest and bravest champion. From that contest one warrior—Princess Diana—triumphed over all and boldly entered the world of mortals. Now her mission is to conquer villainy, defend justice, and restore peace across the globe.

CHAPTER 1

EVIL STIRS

Deep beneath the streets of London, the Servants of Evil marched through an underground crypt. They wore long, black cloaks with hoods and stark white masks to hide their faces.

As minions of an unknown master, the Servants usually committed small crimes. But their meager missions were about to be upgraded. The head of the organization, the Herald, had called them all to the main chamber for an important announcement.

The Servants anxiously filed into the fearsome chamber. The crypt was dark, and the air was damp. Flickering torches lined the walls. Iron chandeliers hung from the ceiling.

BAM! A large wooden door flung open, startling the assembled group.

"He comes!" one of the Servants of Evil cried out.

At last, the Herald came out of his private quarters. He was dressed in a blood-red cloak that hid his face. The crowd stirred with excitement, but one among them didn't share their feelings. Hidden among the Servants of Evil stood a hero in disguise—Wonder Woman.

The Amazon warrior had gotten wind of the group's activities. After suspecting it might be up to something evil, she had secretly invaded its ranks.

Donning the Servants' trademark black cloak and mask, Wonder Woman had slipped into their underground headquarters unnoticed. Now, surrounded by enemies, she waited for the right time to strike.

The Herald gazed out at his followers bowing before him. "Greetings, Servants of Evil!" he exclaimed, his voice echoing through the chamber. "I bring good news to all of you. Our master is very pleased."

"All hail the master!" the group shouted together.

The Herald snapped his fingers. A faithful Servant brought forth a metal case. He opened it to reveal what looked like a gold sword handle with a ruby crystal on one end.

"We have recovered the item our master desires," said the Herald. He took it into his hands and held it high for all to see.

"Simple though this may look," the Herald continued, "many among us have paid a high price to find this precious relic. Let us give thanks to them as we remake the planet."

"But only after we destroy it!" another Servant cried out.

Wonder Woman had heard enough. She whipped off her cloak, revealing her true identity to the crowd.

"You won't be destroying anything today!" the hero barked. "Whatever you're planning is officially *over*."

"How did *you* get in here?!" the Herald asked. "Nothing escapes my notice!"

"Serving your dark master has blinded you, Herald," the Amazon Princess replied. "I urge you to surrender peacefully."

HA! HA! HA! The Herald cackled. "This imposter among us demands our surrender? Teach her a lesson, Servants of Evil. Attack!"

The Servants surrounded Wonder Woman on all sides. "You had your chance," she said, bracing herself for battle.

Two Servants lunged in Wonder Woman's direction, grabbing both of her arms. She used her super-strength to flip them into the air and against the wall behind her.

"Your minds are being controlled," Wonder Woman said. "All of you must fight through the Herald's mental grip with everything you have."

"You're mistaken, Amazon. I control *no one's* mind," the Herald explained. "These Servants of Evil are here because they wish to be. They understand that *true* freedom comes from following a great leader."

Four more Servants charged Wonder Woman. She dropped to the ground and swept her leg across the floor, knocking them all off their feet. As they struggled to recover, more Servants closed in.

Wonder Woman had to act fast. She spotted six iron chandeliers hanging above the chamber. Each one was attached to the ceiling with thick, sturdy chain links.

These chandeliers will help me corral the Servants without hurting them, Wonder Woman thought. She tossed her tiara through the air like a boomerang. It ripped through the chain links in an instant. The iron chandeliers fell onto the Servants, trapping them tightly.

Wonder Woman spotted the gold handle and reached for her magic lasso.

"I'll be taking that!" the hero exclaimed.

Wonder Woman whipped her lasso. In a flash, the item flew out of the Herald's hands and into her own.

The Herald quickly ran down the corridor. The Amazon snagged his foot with her lasso and dragged him back into the chamber.

"You will not stop us," the Herald warned. "We serve a greater power. Our *master* will protect us. You'll see. You'll *all* see."

"Who is your master, and where can I find him?" Wonder Woman asked. "Tell me the truth." She looped her lasso around the Herald and focused its power.

The Herald shook his head. "I do not know. Our leader's identity is a mystery even to us," he said. "We simply follow orders."

Wonder Woman inspected the handle. "What is this?" she asked.

"Something our master has wanted for a very long time. We went to great lengths to find it, though we do not know what it does," said the Herald. "The master tells us it will change the course of history."

"Your master is lying to you," Wonder Woman said, attaching the sword handle to her belt. "I intend to find him and make him pay for his evil ways."

"Hahahahaha!" The Herald laughed as Wonder Woman released her lasso. "You're playing with forces you do not understand."

"I'm not afraid," Wonder Woman said, staring down the Herald. "I suggest you clean up your act. I'll be watching," she warned. "Your master is about to learn his place."

Wonder Woman left the underground base and contacted the London police. They swiftly arrived and took the Servants to jail.

With the sword handle safely in hand, Wonder Woman boarded her Invisible Jet. She fired up its engines and set out for the Museum of Natural History in Washington, D.C. She hoped the museum's new curator, Professor Milton, would be able to shed some light on the mysterious object.

On the way, Wonder Woman realized she might need a helping hand on this mission. She sent her close friend, Steve Trevor, a message to meet her at the museum. Steve was a secret agent with the spy agency known as A.R.G.U.S.

When Wonder Woman arrived at the museum, she found Professor Milton in her office. Milton was a small woman with scraggy, blonde hair and thick, crooked glasses. She wore an oversized sweater and was focused on a tin of cookies in her hand.

"Oh my," Professor Milton gasped, surprised to find Wonder Woman standing there. "I wasn't expecting a guest!"

"I'm sorry, Professor Milton. I didn't mean to startle you," Wonder Woman said. "We haven't had a chance to meet. I am Diana of Themyscira."

"I know who you are, of course. The great Wonder Woman. It's a pleasure." Professor Milton chuckled. She placed the cookie tin on her desk and straightened her glasses. "How can I help you today?"

Wonder Woman revealed the gold handle. "I need help with this," she said.

Professor Milton eyed the item with intense curiosity. "Oh my," she gasped, taking the handle into her hands and carefully inspecting every inch. "Where did you find it?"

"A group calling themselves the Servants of Evil claimed it for a dark and unknown master," said Wonder Woman. "Do you know what it is?"

Professor Milton grinned. "It's something I've been tracking for a very long time. One piece of a very dangerous puzzle. It's the handle of an ancient wand that's been missing for thousands of years," she explained.

Professor Milton pulled an antique scroll from a nearby file cabinet and spread it out across her desk. The scroll showed fearsome monsters ravaging the world, causing chaos and destruction. In the middle of the scene was the wand.

"If the other pieces of the wand are found and assembled, it could destroy the entire planet," Professor Milton said.

"I'll make sure that never happens," said Wonder Woman. "I'll retrieve them at once."

Professor Milton hesitated. "That won't be as easy as you might think," she warned. "The wand has been cursed with a dark and ancient magic."

"Dark magic doesn't frighten me," the hero declared.

Professor Milton smiled. "That's good to hear, because now that the handle has been found, the other pieces have awoken. They know they're being collected and will use their dark magic to fight you."

Milton retrieved two photos from her desk drawer and showed them to Wonder Woman. "These are the other two wand pieces—the shaft and the head. The shaft is simple, with no unusual markings. But the head is tipped with three prongs and a large ruby."

Wonder Woman studied the photos carefully. "Do you know where they are?" she pressed.

"The wand's shaft is at the United Nations museum in New York. It's part of an exhibit on the ancient world. The wand's head is being kept inside a former military base in the mountains of Nevada," Professor Milton explained. "Once they've been collected, give them to me so I can place them in a vault for safekeeping."

"Got it," said Wonder Woman.

"Are you sure you want to go on such a dangerous mission alone, Wonder Woman?" Professor Milton asked. "It will be quite an undertaking, even for a powerful super hero such as yourself."

Before she could answer, Agent Trevor walked into Professor Milton's office.

"I contacted Agent Steve Trevor on my way here," explained Wonder Woman. "He and I have worked together many times before. I trust him with my life."

Steve gave two thumbs up. "And I've always got her back," he said.

"I guess you're prepared for *everything*," Professor Milton remarked. "A true hero."

"She's the best of the best," said Steve. "And I'm not just saying that because she's saved my butt a bunch of times."

"Come, Agent Trevor. I'll brief you on the mission on the way," Wonder Woman said.

"Wait!" Professor Milton exclaimed, grabbing the tin of chocolate chip cookies on her desk. "Have a cookie before you go. I baked them myself. If you don't, I'll just end up throwing them out."

Steve grabbed a cookie and stuffed it in his mouth. "Tasty," he said. "Thanks!"

Professor Milton waved the tin in front of Wonder Woman. "Are you sure I can't tempt you, Princess? They're *extra* fresh."

Wonder Woman smiled kindly. "No thank you, Professor," she replied. "But I appreciate the offer. We'll be back as soon as possible."

"Good luck out there," said Professor Milton as Wonder Woman and Agent Trevor left her office. Then she turned toward a mirror behind her desk and watched her full-body disguise disappear completely. She smiled at the reflection of the purple-haired sorceress clad in green that stared back.

"You're going to need *every* ounce of luck you can get!"

CHAPTER 2

CHAOS AT THE UNITED NATIONS

Wonder Woman and Agent Trevor boarded the Invisible Jet and took off into the sky. A marvel of Amazonian science, the aircraft used stealth technology to mask it from sight.

"I don't think I'll ever get used to riding in this crazy jet of yours. Amazons sure do have a lot of cool stuff," said Steve. "Thanks for inviting me along."

"You and your friends at A.R.G.U.S. have always provided excellent help, which is exactly what this mission requires," Wonder Woman said.

"What's the plan?" asked Steve.

"We're going to track down two pieces of an ancient and powerful wand," the hero explained. She activated a holographic map in the jet's cockpit showing each destination. "The wand's shaft is located at the United Nations. The wand's head is hidden inside a former military base."

"Looks pretty simple to me," said Steve.

"*Looks* can be deceiving. Keep your eyes open and your mind sharp," Wonder Woman said, handing Steve a small box. He eyed it curiously and removed the lid to find a thin rope necklace containing a small pendant.

"Does this turn me invisible? That would be cool," Steve joked. "Though, if I'm being honest, I'd rather be able to fly."

"No superpowers, I'm afraid. The flower inside this Amazonian pendant has been known to protect its wearer," Wonder Woman explained with a smile. "Just think of it as a good luck charm."

"Um, well, I'm not a jewelry guy, but thanks," Steve said. He stuffed the necklace safely into a metal compartment on his utility belt. "So, we're going to grab a couple of old relics, huh? Sounds kind of boring."

"Don't be fooled. We're going up against a dangerous and unpredictable force—dark magic. Be prepared for anything," said Wonder Woman.

"Like I said—*boring!*" Steve exclaimed, throwing his legs up onto the jet's dashboard.

Wonder Woman eyed her friend carefully. Agent Trevor loved to joke around from time to time. But something about his behavior seemed off, and she couldn't quite put her finger on it. "Buckle up," she said. "We'll be there in no time."

The Invisible Jet soon arrived in New York City. Wonder Woman landed outside the United Nations beside a group of tourists.

Steve opened the door of the jet, and the tourists rushed forward to take photos of their favorite super hero.

"Back off! All of you!" Agent Trevor shouted, shooing away the crowd. "Put your cameras away too. Can't you see we're in the middle of something important?!"

Steve turned and whispered in Wonder Woman's ear. "People are so annoying. They're like little *bugs.*"

"That's enough," Wonder Woman whispered. She couldn't believe Steve's rude tone. It wasn't like him at all. She turned to address the crowd with a smile. "Unfortunately, we're here on urgent business and don't have a moment to spare."

Steve released a pained sigh as they made their way toward the building. "I was trying to *protect* you, you know," he growled. "Sorry for being a good friend."

Her friend's odd behavior puzzled Wonder Woman. "Is something wrong, Steve?"

"*Wrong?!*" Steve replied. "I'll tell you what's *wrong*, Princess. I'm sick of dealing with *your* problems. Why can't you just take care of them yourself?"

Wonder Woman wasn't sure how to respond. She'd never seen Steve behave so harshly before.

"I'm always grateful for your help," the hero assured him.

"Yeah, yeah, yeah. *Whatever.* Just drop it, okay!" Steve exclaimed, shaking off his strange feeling. "I guess I just need a nap or something. Let's grab this thing and get out of here."

"You make sure everyone is out of the museum. I'll alert the United Nations that we've arrived," said Wonder Woman. "Stay on guard in case the piece of the wand reacts to us being here."

Inside the U.N. General Assembly Hall, world leaders had gathered to listen to a speech by Secretary-General Acosta. The Secretary-General was a respected friend of Wonder Woman's. As the hero entered the hall, Acosta was urging the United Nations to fight for a peaceful planet.

"Fellow delegates, we must have hope!" Secretary-General Acosta exclaimed. "We must have the courage to stand up to bullies. We mustn't bow before evil. I ask all of you here today to join me in paving a way to a better world. Thank you."

Applause filled the room as the world leaders rose to their feet. The speech was a great success.

Then Secretary-General Acosta spotted Wonder Woman at the back of the hall. She immediately left the podium to greet her.

"Your words are as inspiring as ever, Secretary-General Acosta," said Wonder Woman.

"Thank you, Wonder Woman," the Secretary-General replied. "What brings you here? I'd love for you to meet some of the other delegates."

"I'm afraid I'm not here for a social visit," the hero replied. "A dark force seeks to put together a very powerful weapon. A piece of it, an artifact from the ancient world, is in a U.N. museum exhibit. I'm here to retrieve it before it falls into the wrong hands."

"Say no more," said the Secretary-General. "I'll take you to the exhibit."

HISSSSSSSSS!

Suddenly, a strange green mist flowed out of the air vents and under the doors of the General Assembly Hall. In a matter of moments, the mist blanketed the room. Panic broke out inside the chamber as people scrambled for the exits. But the green mist covered the doors, preventing their escape.

Wonder Woman did her best to control the situation. "Everyone stay calm," she said. "I'll handle this."

A U.N. delegate pointed at Wonder Woman in anger. His eyes had turned purple. "*You're* the one who brought this here!" he shouted. "Heroes like you cause trouble wherever you go!"

"I don't like your tone, mister!" snapped the Secretary-General. Her eyes had turned purple as well. She grabbed a chair and tossed it at the angry delegate. Wonder Woman threw her wrists into the air and used her metal bracelets to deflect the attack.

The chamber erupted into chaos as the delegates began fighting. They tore down flags, toppled desks, and threw chairs at one another. One delegate climbed on stage and ripped down the United Nations crest. "*This* is what we *really* think of peace!" he cried.

"Merciful Minerva," Wonder Woman gasped. "Everyone has gone mad."

A delegate snuck up behind Wonder Woman and smashed a chair across her back. It crumbled to pieces, but the Amazon warrior was unmoved. She took the man by the shoulders and spun him in circles. He became so dizzy, he fell to the ground.

That bizarre mist has given everyone an angry thirst for violence, Wonder Woman thought. *This must be the dark magic that Professor Milton warned me about. I've got to stop these people without hurting them.*

A menacing delegate moved in on Wonder Woman from the front. "I bet *you* want *peace*, don't you?" he asked. "Stupid, stupid, stupid."

Another delegate moved in from behind. "All you *heroes* think about is yourself," she said. "How are we supposed to trust people like *you?*"

Two more delegates flanked her on either side. "Get her!" they cried, charging like a herd of bulls.

Wonder Woman launched herself into the air, and the four attacking delegates crashed into one another, knocking themselves out. As she hovered above the chaos, an idea formed in Wonder Woman's head. She flew to one of the air vents and ripped off its cover.

"I hope this works," she said, twirling her golden lasso at super-speed. The lasso created a vortex of wind that sucked up all of the green mist and safely funneled it through the air vent and out of the building.

The delegates snapped out of their trances, but things didn't return to normal. A tense feeling hung in the air. Everyone had seen each other's dark sides and no longer trusted one another the way they had before.

Secretary-General Acosta looked around the wrecked room, quietly surveying the costly damage.

"Is this the dark magic you spoke of, Wonder Woman?" Acosta asked. "Thank you for what you did to help, but I think it's best if you take what you need and leave."

Wonder Woman understood, but the Secretary-General's words still stung her ears. "Very well," she replied.

Agent Trevor entered the chamber and was shocked by the destruction. "This place is a disaster!" he exclaimed.

Wonder Woman remained silent. She nodded goodbye to Secretary-General Acosta and went to find the piece of the wand.

Steve followed behind. "I cleared the U.N. museum, so we're good to go," he said.

"The wand's shaft knows we're coming for it," said Wonder Woman.

As they entered the museum, Steve sensed Wonder Woman's frustration. "What happened in there that's got you so upset?"

"There's no time to discuss that right now. Let's complete the mission and be on our way," Wonder Woman said. She spotted the wand's shaft under a glass case in the corner. "There it is."

Steve stared at the simple bar of metal and shrugged. "It doesn't look cursed to me," he said. "Hurry up and grab this thing so we can leave. I'm over this dumb mission."

Agent Trevor lifted the top off the case, and Wonder Woman carefully removed the shaft from its display. She gripped it tightly. There was no lightning or thunder. The skies didn't turn black.

"No dark magic," said Steve. "Well, that's good news."

RUMBLE, RUMBLE, RUMBLE!

Steve ran to a nearby window. He watched the ground shake as an enormous sea monster emerged from the East River. It was as big as a skyscraper, covered in bluish-green scales, and had two thin arms complete with razor-sharp claws. Five slimy tentacles lurched up from under its body. The creature craned its dragonlike head in all directions, looking for something to destroy.

"I *had* to go and open my big mouth," Steve said.

CHAPTER 3

SEA MONSTER SMASH

The sea monster reared its head back, opened its mouth, and released an angry cry.

ROAR!!!

The deafening sound shook the city. Windows shattered as buildings swayed back and forth. Frightened citizens scattered in every direction to escape. The beast bared its jagged fangs and cast its hungry gaze upon his ultimate target—Wonder Woman. She now stood on the shore of the East River, planning her next move.

"What is that ugly thing?!" Agent Trevor exclaimed.

"A sea creature from Greek mythology," said Wonder Woman. "I read about it as a child. It's an evil beast that will lay waste to the city if given the chance."

"What are *you* going to do?" asked Steve.

Wonder Woman grinned. "I'm going to stop it," she said, handing the wand shaft to Agent Trevor. "Protect this with your life, Steve. I'll be back."

The Amazon warrior launched herself toward the beast like a speeding bullet. *I'm not about to let that sea monster come ashore and destroy the city,* she thought. *It's time for me to let loose!*

SWACK! Wonder Woman punched the sea creature's snout, knocking it backward.

The creature stumbled, surprised by the powerful attack. It quickly recovered and charged once again. Wonder Woman gave it another swat to the nose.

"Back off!" she exclaimed. "I won't warn you again."

ROAR!!! The angry monster didn't like being told no.

The beast swiped its claws wildly, trying to catch Wonder Woman as she zigzagged through the sky. She was too fast for the snarling sea monster.

The angry creature looked around for something else to destroy. It spotted the Queensboro Bridge bustling with cars—the perfect target. As it made its way toward the bridge, Wonder Woman dove into the water. She grabbed one of the beast's many thrashing tentacles.

Wonder Woman burst from the river with a tentacle slung across her shoulder. "Let's see if this helps keep you away from trouble," she exclaimed. "Hera, give me strength!"

Wonder Woman yanked the creature to a stop, keeping it away from the bridge. But another tentacle shot up from below and whipped the hero in the face. The blow sent her flying. She splashed down in the river and quickly swam to shore.

Steve watched Wonder Woman emerge from the water's edge. "Get your head in the game!" he shouted. "That thing will rip the bridge apart unless *you* do something."

Wonder Woman was nearly exhausted from her struggle with the sea creature, but the battle was far from over. She raced to the bridge where the beast had grabbed a car full of people.

"Drop it!" Wonder Woman shouted. She grabbed the other end of the vehicle, pulled it from the monster's grip, and returned it safely to the roadway.

ROAR!!! The sea creature didn't like having his toys taken away. He bared his claws and began using them to rip apart the bridge. Wonder Woman flew to the very top of the bridge and positioned herself just right.

"This ends now!" she exclaimed, banging her enchanted bracelets together.

CLANG! Wonder Woman's colliding bracelets released a powerful shock wave that blasted the beast away from the bridge. The monster struggled to keep its balance, fighting through a dizzy spell.

The creature is dazed and unaware, Wonder Woman thought. *It's time to end this once and for all.*

The Amazon warrior flew around the sea monster at super-speed, wrapping her magic lasso around it as tightly as she could. She watched as the beast struggled to free itself, but there was no escape.

Before Wonder Woman could haul the monster away, it disappeared in a burst of light as if it had never existed. But the damage had been done. Innocent lives had been put in danger. The entire episode left Wonder Woman confused.

Joining Steve on shore, Wonder Woman wondered if going up against dark magic was the right idea after all.

"Let's hope that sea creature is the worst thing we meet on our quest," she said.

Steve handed the hero the recovered wand shaft. She studied the simple-looking item carefully.

"We'll have to remain extra careful at our next location," Wonder Woman said. "The dark magic that protects these wand pieces isn't going down without a fight."

Steve wasn't sure he wanted to continue on the mission. "What about the people who could've been hurt?" he asked. "You're supposed to be a *hero*, Wonder Woman. You're supposed to keep people *safe*. But your meddling brought the sea monster here. If you hadn't touched that piece of the wand, none of this would have happened."

Steve's sudden shift in perspective confused Wonder Woman. "What are you talking about?" she asked. "According to Professor Milton, if we don't find all of the wand pieces immediately, the whole world might suffer. I can't let that happen."

Steve wasn't convinced.

"That wand is one hundred percent trouble. You want to find the rest of that stupid thing? Fine. You can do it by yourself," Steve said, swiping the wand shaft from her grasp. "I'm taking this piece back to Professor Milton. Then I'm taking a nice long vacation away from you."

"I don't know what's gotten into you, Steve," said Wonder Woman. "But fine. You take that piece to Milton. I'll complete the mission alone."

Wonder Woman parted ways with Steve, but his cruel words stayed with her. *If I bring chaos and destruction with me everywhere I go, perhaps I've failed as a hero,* she thought.

It wasn't like Wonder Woman to doubt herself, but maybe Steve was right. Maybe she wasn't the champion of peace she thought she was.

Wonder Woman boarded the Invisible Jet and took off for the former military base in the Nevada mountains. She put the plane on autopilot and made her way toward the back of the vehicle.

Using advanced Amazonian technology, Wonder Woman opened a communication portal to Themyscira, the island she once called home. In a swirl of light, Hippolyta, Queen of the Amazons, appeared.

"Hello, Diana," the queen said with a warm smile. "It's good to see you."

"Greetings, Mother," said Wonder Woman.

Queen Hippolyta noticed her daughter's nervousness. "Is everything okay, my dear?" she asked. "You look troubled."

"Mother, am I worthy of my title?" Wonder Woman asked.

Hippolyta chuckled softly to herself. "Oh, Diana. Don't say such silly things. You are *Wonder Woman,* the Amazon's messenger of peace in the outside world," she said. "What could possibly make you doubt yourself?"

"I took on a quest," Wonder Woman said. "One that involves dark magic."

"Dark magic can cloud our thoughts and poison our minds," said Queen Hippolyta.

"Innocent people were put in harm's way because of me," Wonder Woman explained. "Maybe it's time I pass the responsibility on to someone worthier than I."

"There is no one worthier than you, my daughter," said Queen Hippolyta. "The life of a hero is never easy, Diana. But without your selfless heroism, the world would be a very different place. Don't doubt yourself. People need you to be strong."

Wonder Woman carefully considered her mother's words. They were exactly what she needed to hear. "I suppose you're right. Being a hero isn't always easy," she said. "Thank you, Mother."

Hippolyta motioned to the suit of Amazonian armor hanging nearby. "You might consider wearing your armor next time. It will bring you added protection against the forces of dark magic. May the gods be with you, Diana," Queen Hippolyta said, fading away.

One more piece of the wand to go, Wonder Woman thought.

CHAPTER 4

SNAKE ATTACK

Wonder Woman stood before a giant steel door set in the side of a mountain. She wore her Amazonian battle armor and had a fierceness in her eyes.

With her sword and shield in hand, she was prepared to do whatever it took to find the final piece of the wand. But there was no telling what dangers awaited her inside the abandoned military base.

Though it had once been an active military bunker, the fortress now served as an unmanned storage facility. Locked inside were strange artifacts and items of power. They'd been placed there for protection from the villains who'd use them for evil.

The metal door was a foot thick with no one on the other side to open it. For an ordinary person, opening such a door would be impossible. Thankfully, Wonder Woman was anything but ordinary.

There's no time to waste, she thought. *I've got a mission to complete.*

Wonder Woman dug her fingers beneath the metal door and tore it off using her incredible super-strength. As she entered the cavernous fortress, she noticed the mountain had been hollowed out to make room for the thousands of items it stored.

Planes and spaceships hung from the ceiling. Mysterious vehicles sat dormant, covered by tarps. And there were hundreds of crates spread out and piled on top of one another. Clearly, finding the head of the wand wasn't going to be easy.

Before Wonder Woman could begin her search, a mysterious voice called out from above. "Are you worthy, Diana?" it asked. "Are you sure you're a real hero?"

My mind is playing tricks on me, Wonder Woman thought. *The dark magic that protects the wand's head wants to throw me off my game.* She shook off the taunts and began searching the crates, one after the other.

"Why isn't Agent Trevor helping you?" asked the mysterious voice. "Have you lost his trust? Tsk, tsk, tsk. Perhaps it's time you finally gave up."

That voice sounds strangely familiar, Wonder Woman thought. *But I can't let it get to me. I have to stay focused on the task at hand.*

After searching for more than an hour, Wonder Woman found a crate covered in familiar writing. "These symbols are ancient Greek," she said. "I wonder if this box contains the item I've been searching for."

Wonder Woman tore off the cover to find the jewel-topped head of the wand. A feeling of relief washed over her body. But before she could take the piece of the wand, a slithering snake tail knocked the crate from her grasp.

"Great Zeus!" Wonder Woman exclaimed. The tail grabbed her around the waist and slammed her against the cavern wall over and over again. The mountain shook with each forceful blow. Eventually, the tail loosened, and she dropped to the ground.

Wonder Woman looked up to find that the tail belonged to Echidna, the Mother of Monsters. She was an enormous half-woman, half-snake creature from ancient myth. Before Wonder Woman could catch her breath, Echidna used her tail to furiously toss crates at her. They soon covered the Amazon Princess completely.

BOOM!

Down but not out, Wonder Woman quickly burst free from the makeshift prison. She rubbed her eyes and brushed her shoulders off.

Echidna was ready to attack again. In ancient times, she charmed her victims and then ate them whole. Wonder Woman wasn't about to let that happen.

"Do your worst!" the hero shouted, raising her sword. "I won't be taken down so easily."

Echidna opened her mouth and shot a stream of poisonous venom in Wonder Woman's direction. The Amazon warrior swiftly raised her shield, blocking the attack. The warm venom sizzled as it splashed against Wonder Woman's protective armor.

"How about a taste of your own vile medicine?" Wonder Woman asked. She tossed the venom-covered shield toward Echidna, striking the serpentine monster in the face.

SCREECH!

Echidna didn't like that one bit. She slapped her snake tail on the cavern floor repeatedly. Each blow shook the mountain.

Time was running out. Wonder Woman had to retrieve her prize. As if reading her mind, Echidna reached into the crate and grabbed the wand head. Wrestling it from her grasp wasn't going to be easy.

"You'll never win, Amazon," taunted the mysterious voice. "You're far too weak. You're much too feeble. Give up now or face embarrassment later."

At last, Wonder Woman figured out exactly who the voice belonged to.

Circe! she thought. *It all makes sense now. Circe is the one who cursed the wand with dark magic in the first place. That ancient witch is up to something. I need to grab the final piece of the wand before it falls into her hands.*

SCREECH!

Echidna lunged toward Wonder Woman. The hero ducked and rolled to avoid her.

"Our battle is at an end, monster!" Wonder Woman exclaimed. She tossed her golden lasso around the giant snake-woman and held on tight.

As Echidna struggled to free herself, her tricky tail slithered up behind Wonder Woman and coiled around her body. The hero dropped her magic lasso as she became trapped completely.

"Let this be a lesson for you, Wonder Woman," the voice hissed. "Never play with dark magic."

Wonder Woman summoned every ounce of super-strength and burst free from Echidna's deadly grasp. She grabbed the monster's squirming tail and tied it in a knot.

"That should keep you busy for a while," Wonder Woman said.

Echidna was far from defeated. She bared her sharp talons and lurched toward Wonder Woman. The Amazon warrior deflected the attack with a block from her shield.

Echidna reared back in anger. She swiped her claws once more, but Wonder Woman stood ready. The Amazon grabbed the creature by both wrists and squeezed as hard as she could.

SCREECH! Echidna cried out in agony. Wonder Woman picked up her lasso and moved into a ready position.

"You put up quite a fight, creature," Wonder Woman growled. "But you'll always lose when you underestimate the power of an Amazon."

Wonder Woman raised her sword into the air and lunged toward Echidna. Before she could strike, the giant snake-monster disappeared completely, as if she'd never even existed.

"You won't win, Circe!" Wonder Woman exclaimed. "Not now. Not ever."

* * *

With the final piece of the wand in hand, Wonder Woman rushed back to the Museum of Natural History. She landed her Invisible Jet on the museum's roof and raced to meet Professor Milton.

Dashing into Milton's office, Wonder Woman cleared away a stack of papers on the professor's desk. She set down the head of the wand for examination.

Professor Milton's eyes lit up like a Christmas tree. "Is that what I think it is?" she asked with devilish excitement.

"It's the final piece of the puzzle," said Wonder Woman.

"But how on earth did you get it?" asked Professor Milton.

"I defeated the mythical Echidna. But that's not all. I also heard the sorceress Circe's voice calling out to me during the battle. This must be Circe's wand, which she, herself, cursed with dark magic."

"You don't say," said Professor Milton with a sly smile.

"Yes," continued Wonder Woman. "We must be extra careful. If Circe gets wind that the wand pieces have been collected, she may try to take back what was once hers."

"I wouldn't worry," Milton said. Then she grabbed the head of the wand and clutched it tight. "Everything will be just fine now that I finally have what I want."

Wonder Woman spotted the gold handle on Professor Milton's desk. It was sitting next to the wand shaft from the United Nations.

"We need to get all of these pieces into your vault," Wonder Woman said. "It's the only way to protect them."

"Oh, I forgot to tell you. There's been a little change in plans," said Professor Milton. "We won't be doing *any* of that."

"I don't understand," Wonder Woman said. "What are you talking about?"

Professor Milton furiously snapped the pieces of the wand together. "I suppose I don't need this anymore," she said, tapping the wand against her palm.

POOF!

In an explosion of purple flames, Professor Milton transformed into her true identity. Circe, the Goddess of Dark Magic, now stood before Wonder Woman.

"*Surprise!*" Circe exclaimed. "Miss me?"

CHAPTER 5

DARKNESS REIGNS

Without knowing it, Wonder Woman had been helping one of her worst enemies all along. The discovery left the Amazon Princess in a state of shock.

"It's been a long time, Diana," Circe said with a sneer.

"Not long enough, Circe," growled Wonder Woman.

Circe stroked her long, purple hair and smiled at the hero.

"Professor Milton served her purpose, but it feels so *good* to finally be *myself* again," the villain said with a giggle. "Thank you for helping me put together my wand. I hope it still works after all this time."

Circe pointed the wand at Wonder Woman and fired a bolt of dark magic energy. **SHAZACK!**

Wonder Woman threw her hands in the air, using her bracelets to deflect the attack.

"You are a lot better at defending yourself than my Servants of Evil," said Circe.

"You were the dark master they served, weren't you?" asked Wonder Woman.

"Guilty as charged. Without me they were just homeless and broke," Circe said. "I gave those weaklings a purpose. I promised them power as long as they followed their leader."

"You manipulated them," said Wonder Woman. "How could you?"

"Oh please! They needed something to believe in. I simply gave it to them. In exchange, they did what I said," Circe explained. "That is until you showed up. Normally I would've been upset with you for meddling in my plans. But then you brought the wand handle right to my doorstep!"

"And you manipulated *me*," Wonder Woman said.

"Maybe just a little bit," Circe sneered. "Your friend, Agent Trevor, helped. I couldn't have done it without him." She eyed the tin of cookies sitting on the desk. "Hungry? I cursed them with dark magic."

"You poisoned Steve's mind," said Wonder Woman. "That's why he acted so strangely."

"I knew if I could get you to doubt yourself, you'd be putty in my hands," Circe revealed. "Agent Trevor was also kind enough to unleash my poison mist pellets at the United Nations. I magically slipped them into his utility belt when he wasn't looking. How does it feel to have the whole world against you, Wonder Woman?"

Circe fired off another bolt of dark magic energy. **SHAZACK!**

Wonder Woman pulled her shield from her back and blocked the blast.

"Tell me where Steve is, or I'll bring the fury of the gods upon you," the hero said. "Do not make me ask you a second time."

Circe waved her wand. In a burst of purple smoke, Steve suddenly appeared. He was trapped inside a prison cell, confused by his surroundings.

"Where am I?" Steve wondered aloud. "What happened to me?"

"Awww. He doesn't *remember.* That's probably for the best. You betrayed your friend, *Steve,*" Circe said. "You planted seeds of doubt in her mind and made her feel like a failure. *You* helped destroy Wonder Woman."

Steve couldn't believe what he was hearing. "Is Circe right, Wonder Woman?" he asked. "Is it *my* fault we're in this mess?"

"Circe poisoned your mind. You weren't in control of yourself," Wonder Woman explained. She directed her growing anger toward Circe. "No more lies and deception, witch. Tell me what you want."

"World domination in the long term. In the short term, I want your *weapons* and *armor.* I want you to bow before me in total surrender," Circe revealed. "How about it?"

"Never!" Wonder Woman barked.

"Then you leave me no choice," Circe said. She swirled the wand through the air and produced a new creature of myth. The enormous beast had red eyes, dark gray skin, and a handful of tentacles. A pair of scaly wings burst from its back. "This is Echidna's husband, Typhon, the Father of Monsters," she said. "Be nice and say hello, Typhon."

ROAR!!!

Typhon's cry shattered all of the glass display cases inside the museum.

"Isn't he fun?" asked Circe. "Show Wonder Woman how you attack, boy."

Typhon smashed through the museum wall, crashing onto the street outside. He grabbed a parked car, picked it up, and tossed it into the air like a toy.

I have to act fast, Wonder Woman thought.

The Amazon raced to the scene, swiftly catching the vehicle before it fell to the ground. Innocent bystanders ran for their lives as Typhon continued his rampage.

Wonder Woman charged the monster, striking him in the face with her shield. At the same moment, a fleet of A.R.G.U.S. troopers arrived on the scene. They'd been sent to stop Typhon before he destroyed Washington, D.C.

"Go away, swine!" Circe shouted. With a wave of her wand, she turned all of the A.R.G.U.S. troopers into squealing piglets. "That's *much* better."

Wonder Woman raised her sword to deliver the final blow. But before she could strike, Typhon suddenly disappeared.

"He's too boring," Circe sneered. "But don't worry. I've got another trick up my sleeve that you'll *really* like." She held her wand tightly, feeling its raw power course through her entire body. In an instant, the sky turned pitch black. Red lightning bolts filled the clouds.

Circe pointed her wand and zapped Steve with dark magic. His prison cell dissolved, and his clothes ripped as his body tripled in size. Thick clumps of hair sprouted from his skin, and his fingertips became sharp talons. Now a half-man, half-animal Bestiamorph, Steve was completely under Circe's control. He snarled at Wonder Woman, slowly inching toward her.

"Circe, what have you done?!" exclaimed Wonder Woman.

"I made him *better*," Circe replied.

The Bestiamorph charged Wonder Woman. She looked deep into its eyes and saw Steve struggling to understand what was happening to him. Before she could act, the creature grabbed the Amazon, pinned her on the ground, and snarled in her face. She felt helpless against it.

If I don't do something, one of my closest friends may end up destroying me against his will, she thought. *Now I know what I must do.*

"Stop!" Wonder Woman shouted. "I surrender, Circe. End this madness."

The Bestiamorph paused.

"You'll be my slave forever?" Circe asked.

"Yes," Wonder Woman said softly. "I have only one condition. Change Agent Trevor back and allow me to say goodbye to him. Only then will I be yours to control."

Circe flicked her wand, and Steve shed his beastly body. As he become human again, he released Wonder Woman and collapsed to the ground.

"Lay your weapons at my feet," Circe said. "I want them all."

Wonder Woman took her armor off, piece by piece, and laid it on the ground in front of Circe. She placed her sliver bracelets, golden tiara, and magic lasso beside her shield and sword as well.

"Such gorgeous Amazonian handiwork," Circe said, gazing at her prizes. "Helpless and without your weapons is a good look on you, Diana."

"Don't do this," Steve pleaded. "You can't let Circe win. That's not the Wonder Woman I know. That's not who you are! You're a fighter. You never give up."

"Circe is more powerful than I am. This is for the best," Wonder Woman said. As she moved closer to Steve, the look on her face changed. She was up to something.

"Reach into your belt and give me the pendant," Wonder Woman whispered.

"Huh?" muttered Steve.

"The pendant I gave you for good luck," Wonder Woman whispered. "I need it."

Steve fished the pendant out of his utility belt and secretly passed it to Wonder Woman. "You're going to need more than *this* if you want to defeat Circe," he said.

"Just watch," Wonder Woman whispered.

Circe was growing anxious. "Enough with the sappy goodbyes," she grumbled. "Get over here and bow before me, Diana. Stop wasting my time."

Wonder Woman slowly made her way toward Circe. As she got closer, the villainess began to lose her balance. Circe waved her wand, but it only produced a small spark.

"What's going on here?" the villain asked. "My magic is fading."

Wonder Woman showed off Steve's pendant. "This contains an ancient flowering herb called Moly," she explained. "In modern times, it has been used for good luck. But its original purpose was . . ."

"To disrupt my power," Circe growled. "Get it away from me!" She pointed her wand at Wonder Woman, but the Amazon warrior kicked it out of her hand before she could use it.

"No!" Circe exclaimed. She chased the wand, scrambling to grab her most prized possession as it rolled away.

Wonder Woman leaped forward and stomped on the wand. She smashed it to pieces, breaking all of Circe's dark spells. She then ensnared the sorceress in her magic lasso and bound her to the pendant.

The charm instantly sapped Circe's remaining power. The conflict finally came to an end.

Wonder Woman checked Circe to make sure she was secure. "I'm taking you to Themyscira where you'll face Amazonian justice," she said. "Then I'll return to help clean up the messes you've made."

Steve picked up the pieces of the wand and placed them in his utility belt. "I'll bring these back to A.R.G.U.S. where they'll be locked away forever. I've had enough of this dark magic."

"Thank you, Steve," said Wonder Woman.

Steve was embarrassed by his behavior toward Wonder Woman. Even though he had been under Circe's control, he felt bad about treating his friend so poorly.

"I'm sorry I was so cruel to you, Diana," Steve said. "I hope you'll forgive me."

"You're already forgiven," said Wonder Woman. "Evil comes in many forms, even in that of a friend. We must keep our eyes open and our minds sharp. Stay strong so evil doesn't rise again and take power."

Steve rubbed his belly. "And don't eat any more funny cookies," he said with a grin.

CIRCE

BASE:
Aeaea

SPECIES:
Olympian

OCCUPATION:
Sorceress

HEIGHT:
5 feet 11 inches

WEIGHT:
145 pounds

EYES:
Blue

HAIR:
Purple

POWERS/ABILITIES:
Nearly limitless magical power, including the power to transform mortal beings into animals. She also has the power to project her voice, image, and energy bolts over long distances.

BIOGRAPHY:

Circe is an ancient sorceress who has a mischievous spirit and a flair for the dramatic. The villain practices the art of dark magic, though she's far from perfect at using it fully. Her magical abilities include changing people into animals, projecting her voice, firing magical energy blasts, and teleporting between dimensions. Over the millennia, Circe has taken many different forms in order to trick people into doing her bidding. One never knows where she might pop up next.

· Circe hates Wonder Woman and everything she stands for. She has spent a large amount of time plotting against the Amazon Princess and believes it's the hero's fault she has yet to become a villainous powerhouse.

· Circe loves nothing more than to humiliate others. That may be why animal transformation is one of her magical specialties. More often than not, those who cross her find themselves turned into pigs!

· Circe may have magic on her side, but Wonder Woman has a little magic of her own. The Amazon warrior's silver bracelets are the perfect defense against Circe's sorcery. They allow Wonder Woman to block magic, preventing damage and transformation.

BIOGRAPHIES

Brandon T. Snider has authored more than 75 books featuring pop culture icons such as Captain Picard, Transformers, and the Muppets. Additionally, he's written books for Cartoon Network favorites such as *Adventure Time*, *Regular Show*, and *Powerpuff Girls*. He's best known for the top-selling *DC Comics Ultimate Character Guide* and the award-winning *Dark Knight Manual*. Brandon lives in New York City and is a member of the Writer's Guild of America.

Luciano Vecchio was born in 1982 and is based in Buenos Aires, Argentina. As a freelance artist for many projects at Marvel and DC Comics, his work has been seen in print and online around the world. He has illustrated many DC Super Heroes books for Capstone, and some of his recent comic work includes *Beware the Batman*, *Green Lantern: The Animated Series*, *Young Justice*, *Ultimate Spider-Man*, and his creator owned web-comic, *Sereno*.

GLOSSARY

antique (an-TEEK)—a very old object that is valuable because it is rare or beautiful

artifact (AR-tuh-fakt)—an object used in the past that was made by people

autopilot (AW-toh-py-luht)—a device that automatically controls an aircraft

bystander (BYE-stan-dur)—someone who is at a place where something happens to someone else

crypt (KRIPT)—a chamber used as a grave

delegate (DEL-uh-guht)—someone who represents other people at a meeting

dormant (DOR-muhnt)—not active

imposter (im-POSS-tur)—someone who pretends to be something he or she is not

pendant (PEN-duhnt)—a hanging ornament, often worn on a necklace

relic (REL-ik)—something that has survived from the past

technology (tek-NOL-uh-jee)—a piece of equipment or machinery developed with the use of scientific knowledge

vortex (VOHR-tex)—air moving in a circular motion

DISCUSSION QUESTIONS

1. Wonder Woman trusted Steve because he's one of her closest friends. Who is a friend you trust? What are some positive qualities that make him or her trustworthy?

2. Wonder Woman gives Steve the pendant as a good luck charm. Do you believe in good luck charms? Explain why or why not.

3. Circe used dark magic to make Wonder Woman doubt herself. Describe a time when you doubted your abilities. Explain how you overcame your feelings of uncertainty.

WRITING PROMPTS

1. Imagine you had a magic wand like Circe's. What would you do with it? Write a short story about your adventures with your magic wand.

2. Circe turned Steve into a half-human, half-animal Bestiamorph. Draw a picture of what you think Steve looked like in this monstrous form and label his most unique features.

3. At the end of the story, Wonder Woman promises to take Circe to the island of Themyscira to face Amazonian justice. Write a new chapter that shows what happens when they get there. Does Circe go to prison or does she escape? You decide!